THE 143-STOREY TREEHOUSE

Andy Griffiths lives in a 143-storey treehouse with his friend Terry and together they make funny books, just like the one you're holding in your hands right now. Andy writes the words and Terry draws the pictures. If you'd like to know more, read this book (or visit www.andygriffiths.com.au).

Terry Denton lives in a 143-storey treehouse with his friend Andy and together they make funny books, just like the one you're holding in your hands right now. Terry draws the pictures and Andy writes the words. If you'd like to know more, read this book (or visit www.terrydenton.com.au).

Climb higher every time
with the Treehouse series

ANDY GRIFFITHS

THE 143-STOREY TREEHOUSE

BY

ANDY GRIFFITHS

& TERRY DENTON

MACMILLAN CHILDREN'S BOOKS

First published 2021 by Pan Macmillan Australia Pty Limited

First published in the UK 2021 by Macmillan Children's Books
an imprint of Pan Macmillan
The Smithson, 6 Briset Street, London EC1M 5NR
EU representative: Macmillan Publishers Ireland Ltd, 1st Floor,
The Liffey Trust Centre, 117–126 Sheriff Street Upper
Dublin 1, D01 YC43
Associated companies throughout the world
www.panmacmillan.com

ISBN 978-1-5290-4787-5

1 3 5 7 9 8 6 4 2

A CIP catalogue record for this book is available from the British Library.

Typeset in 14/18 Minion Pro by Seymour Designs
Printed and bound by CPI Group (UK) Ltd, Croydon CR0 4YY

CONTENTS

CHAPTER 1

THE 143-STOREY TREEHOUSE

Hi, my name is Andy.

This is my friend Terry.

We live in a tree.

Well, when I say 'tree', I mean treehouse. And when I say 'treehouse', I don't just mean any old treehouse—I mean a 143-*storey* treehouse. (It used to be a 130-storey treehouse, but we've added another 13 storeys.)

So what are you waiting for?
Come on up!

We've got a word-o-matic (it knows every word in the whole world!),

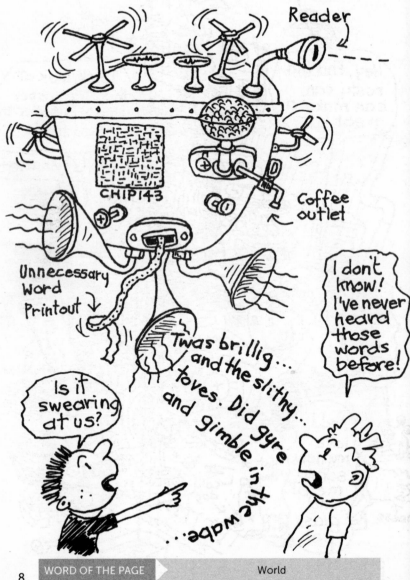

WORD OF THE PAGE World

a recycling depot,

a wrecking ball,

A round object, easily confused with a head

11

a camping ground,

WORD OF THE PAGE ▶ Ground

a too-hard basket,

a SUPER BIG STUFF storey,

a baked bean geyser (it erupts on the hour, every hour),

a Ye Olde Worlde Historical Village,

a fish milkshake bar (we hate them, but the penguins love them!),

WORD OF THE PAGE Fish

a complaining room,

a spooky graveyard (where it's always midnight, even in the middle of the day),

WORD OF THE PAGE ▶ Graveyard

a toffee-apple orchard guarded by a kind scarecrow,

and a deep, dark cave with a real live fire-breathing dragon (well, we haven't actually ever seen it, but we're pretty sure it's there).

As well as being our home, the treehouse is where we make books together. I write the words and Terry draws the pictures.

As you can see, we've been doing this for quite a while now.

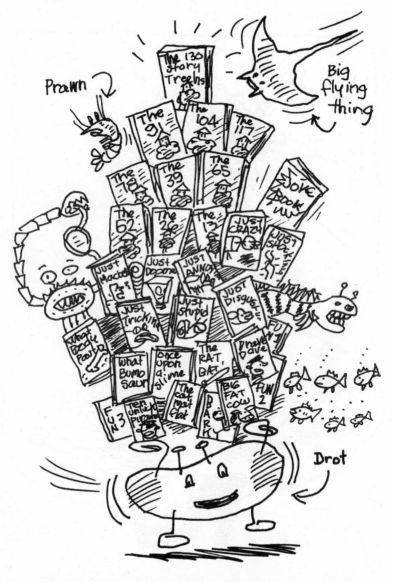

It's not always easy. Sometimes we have unexpected visitors …

27

but we always get our book done in the end.

CHAPTER 2

QUAZJEX?!

Letters

chomp! chomp!

If you're like most of our readers you're probably wondering what my favourite word in the whole world is. Well, it's *Andy*, of course! It's the best word with the best letters.

'**A** is for Awesome,

N is for Never-wrong,

D is for Dazzling and

Y is for—'

'Your turn,' says Terry.

'Please don't interrupt me, Terry,' I say.

'But it's your turn!'

Excuse me, readers. As you can see, I'm in the middle of playing a game of Scrabble with Terry. Now let me see … Hang on, what's *that* word?

'*Quazjex?*' I say. 'What's that? That's not a word!'

DEFINITION   *Awesome, never-wrong, dazzling etc.*

'Yes it is,' says Terry.

'What does it mean?' I say.

'It means I win,' says Terry. 'Because I used up all my letters and I got 260 points!'

'It means you *cheated*!' I say. 'There's no such word as *quazjex*.'

'Yes there is,' says Terry.

'Prove it then,' I say. 'Use it in a sentence.'

'Easy,' says Terry. 'I got a new pet axolotl and its name is Quazjex!'

'That doesn't count,' I say. 'You can't use proper nouns in Scrabble.'

'What about your name?' says Terry. 'That's a proper noun, and you've used it over and over. If you can have *Andy*, then I can have *Quazjex*.'

'Andy may be a proper noun,' I say, 'but at least it's a *proper* proper noun.'

'So is Quazjex,' says Terry.

'Why don't we let the word-o-matic decide?' I say. 'Hey, word-o-matic, is Quazjex a real name?'

The word-o-matic repeats the word.

Quazjex! Quazjex! Quazjex!

Smoke starts pouring out of the machine.

Does not compute. Does not compute. Does not compute. Does not compute. Does not—

'Uh-oh, it's going to blow!' I say. 'Duck!'

Terry and I throw ourselves to the floor and cover our heads.

WORD OF THE PAGE > Fool

SINGLE... JANGLE

A APPLE BYTE MIGHT HEIGHT G...

FAT SAT UPON SEAT WHEAT P...

..K BARK OINK OINK OINK CHIRP WO...

... POOL WOOL COOL RULE DUAL TO...

...E DAPPLE DIDDLEY SWAN PHOP DIP DOPP...

IGGLE **IGLE** MIGGLE TIGGLE SNIGGLE WIGGLE

... KOALA DUMBBELL LIL... PANCAKE B...

TINY SMALLISH BIG GIANT MASSIVE... GINORMOUS

IMO CART EVE JOHN JO... MARC...

OOP DOOP POOP MO...

TODAY GIRL BOY... **GLOOP**

GET GET G... DOLLOP

...ER MUSHROOM... GET GET **GET** DON'T

HUMBLE FL... ARMADILLO GET GET **GET**

BLAM! MILK HAM KLUNK TW...

...OJANGLE MANG...

FREE GUTS ZOOOO COW BOW WOOOH

PAVLOVA DIG

...OO

'Now look what you've done!' I say. 'Your fake word made the word-o-matic explode!'

'Yeah,' says Terry, laughing. 'There are words everywhere!'

'IT'S NOT FUNNY!' I shout. 'It's going to take FOREVER to get all these words back into the machine! There are at least five thousand of them!'

'I know,' says Terry, 'and some of them are pretty funny, too. Look at this one: *flumadiddle*. Hilarious! I wonder what it means?'

WORD OF THE PAGE ▶   Flumadiddle

'Well, we'll never know, will we?' I yell. 'Because you broke the word-o-matic! You break everything!'

'Calm down, Andy,' says Terry. 'I can fix it.'

'I AM CALM!' I shout.

'No you're not,' says Terry. 'You're really angry.'

'I'M NOT ANGRY!' I shout even louder.

'Yes you are,' says Terry. 'In fact, now I think about it, you've been angry a lot lately. You've been losing your temper over really little things.'

'No I haven't!' I say. 'I NEVER lose my temper!'

'You're losing it right now!' says Terry.

'And you lost it yesterday, too,' says Terry.

'And the day before …

and the day before that as well.'

'Maybe you're right,' I say. 'Maybe I need one of those things where you go away and relax and take it easy … um … I can't remember what they're called.'

Holiday is the word you're looking for, says the word-o-matic.

'Thanks, word-o-matic!' I say. 'And yes, a holiday would be nice, but I don't know if a holiday is the answer. I mean, our last holiday was a disaster.'

WORD OF THE PAGE ▶ Holiday

'And the one before that was even worse.'

'And the one before that was the worst of all!'

'We don't have to go to any of *those* lands,' says Terry. 'We'll keep it simple. Why don't we go camping at our new camping ground? There'll be no hot-cheese whirlpools, no fiery pits and no horseheads. Just you and me resting, relaxing and sitting by the campfire.'

'Sounds good,' I say. 'Let's get packing.'

WORD OF THE PAGE   Campfire

'No need,' says Terry. 'I've already packed
everything in our all-terrain treehouse truck.'

'Wait,' I say. 'Have you packed the tent?'

'Check,' he says.

'Have you packed the food—including the
marshmallow machine?'

'Check, check.'

'Have you packed the axe, the portable basketball ring, totem-tennis pole and racquets, yo-yos, board games, books, comics, rocket boosters, kitchen sink, spare kitchen sink and emergency replacement spare kitchen sink?'

CHECK
CHECK
CHECK
CHECK!

'Check, check, check, CHECK!' says Terry impatiently.
'Then I guess we're ready!' I say.

We jump in the treehouse truck and are about to take off when …

'I wonder who that could be?' says Terry, reaching to accept the call on our 3D video phone.

'Wait!' I say. 'It's probably Mr Big Nose. If we don't answer it, he won't be able to remind us about our next book and we'll be able to have our holiday in peace!'

'You've already answered it, you nincompoops!' says Mr Big Nose. 'I can hear every word you're saying! What's this about a holiday? You've got a book due at the end of this week!'

'But we need a break,' I say.

'I'll give you a break all right,' says Mr Big Nose. 'I'll break every bone in your bodies if you don't get your book in on time.'

WORD OF THE PAGE ▶ Nincompoops

'But we're all packed and ready to leave,' says Terry. 'We're going for a nice relaxing holiday on our new camping ground level.'

'That's perfect,' says Mr Big Nose. 'You'll have plenty of free time to do your book! And I've just had a great idea! I'll get *GO AWAY!* magazine to send a reporter and a photographer to do an exclusive feature story on your holiday. It will be GREAT publicity!'

'That doesn't sound like much of a holiday,' I say.

'You'll have a permanent holiday in the monkey house if you don't do what I tell you!' Mr Big Nose threatens.

'I hate monkeys!' says Terry.

'Then you'd better get your book done *and* give *GO AWAY!* magazine your full cooperation!' shouts Mr Big Nose. 'Now, go away—oh, and by the way, HAPPY HOLIDAYS!'

He hangs up.

'Quick,' I say. 'There's no time to lose. If we leave right now, we can get away before the *GO AWAY!* crew gets here and have a holiday with just the two of us like we planned.'

WORD OF THE PAGE ▶ Quick

CHAPTER 3

ARE WE THERE YET?

'Are we there yet?' says Terry.

'Are you kidding?' I say. 'We only just left. Look, we haven't even passed Edward Scooperhands' ice-cream parlour yet.'

'Can we stop and get an ice-cream?' says Terry. 'I really want an ice-cream!'

'So do I,' I say. 'But I want a holiday more.'

'And you'll get one,' says Terry, 'right after we stop for an ice-cream. Besides, a holiday's not a holiday without ice-cream.'

WORD OF THE PAGE   Ice-cream

Terry's right, of course. We stop and go inside.

I choose a choc-banana, new bicycle, flying monkey combo, but Terry, as usual, is having trouble deciding.

'Hmm,' he says. 'We've got a long drive ahead of us so I think I'll have one with the lot, please, Edward.'

'A long drive?' says Edward. 'Where are you off to?'
    'We're going on a camping holiday,' says Terry.

'A holiday!' says Edward. 'Wow, I haven't had a holiday since … um … actually, I don't think I've ever had a holiday.'
    'Why don't you come with us?' says Terry.
    'I'd love to,' says Edward. 'But if I go on holiday who would run the ice-cream parlour?'

'Nobody!' says Terry. 'But it won't matter, because Andy and I won't be here!'

'Then I accept!' says Edward. 'I'll just grab my portable ice-cream vendor tray and be right with you!'

Edward jumps into the back seat and we take off again. I was hoping it would just be Terry and me, but Edward is good company—and he does have a portable ice-cream tray—so I don't really mind.

We drive for a few more minutes.

'Are we there yet?' says Terry.

'No,' I sigh, 'we're only just passing Mary Lollipoppins' lollipop shop.'

'Can we stop and get a lollipop?' says Terry.

'I don't think that's a good idea,' I say. 'We'll never get to the camping ground if we keep stopping every five minutes.'

'I don't want to stop every five minutes,' says Terry. 'I just want to stop and get a lollipop.'

'Me too,' says Edward. 'And Mary is such a nice lollipop-serving robot!'

'Oh, all right then,' I say, 'but this is definitely the last stop.'

We get out and choose lollipops. I get a futuristic one that has flashing lights and Terry gets a cactus lollipop with spikes all over it. And Edward gets—what else?—an ice-cream-flavoured lollipop.

'Is *ice-cream* even a flavour?' says Terry.

'It certainly is,' says Mary. 'And one of the nicest. What are you all up to today?'

'We're going on a camping holiday!' says Terry.

'Oh, how wonderful,' says Mary. 'I haven't been on a holiday since … um … actually, I don't think I've ever been on a holiday!'

'I've never been on a holiday either!' says Edward. 'Why don't you come with us?'

'I'd love to,' says Mary. 'But who will look after the lollipop shop while I'm gone?'

'Nobody!' says Edward. 'But it won't matter, because Andy and Terry will be on holiday, too!'

'In that case,' says Mary, 'I'll come. I'll just get my portable lollipop vendor tray and be right with you.'

We go back to the truck, but Terry has packed so much stuff that there's not enough room for Mary *and* her lollipop tray.

'Oh,' she sighs. 'I won't be able to come after all.'

'Yes you will!' says Terry. 'I packed a spare trailer—you can ride in that!'

'And I'll join you!' says Edward. 'A trailer ride sounds like fun!'

So Terry hitches the trailer to the back of the truck, and Mary and Edward get in. Then we set off again and don't stop until we get there.

Well, when I say 'don't stop until we get there', I mean we don't stop except to pick up The Trunkinator,

Boxing glove

the kind scarecrow,

the three wise owls,

A boxing elephant

Pinchy McPhee,

Fancy Fish

WORD OF THE PAGE ▶ Fancy

and a whole bunch of noisy penguins.

'That's it!' I say to Terry. 'If we keep stopping, we'll *never* get there!'

'You're right, Andy,' says Terry. 'No more stopping. Hey, look up ahead! Hitchhikers! We should stop and give them a ride.'

'No way!' I say, looking at the two people waiting by the side of the branch up ahead. 'We already have too many passengers!'

'But they're hitchhikers,' says Terry. 'How will they get to where they're going if we don't give them a lift?'

'All right,' I say. 'We can stop, but this is absolutely the very last time.'

We pull up next to a man holding a camera and a woman holding a notebook.

'Hi,' says Terry. 'Where are you off to?'

'The camping ground,' says the man. 'We're going on a camping holiday.'

'What a coincidence!' says Terry. 'So are we! My name is Terry and this is Andy.'

pineapple

Sto
playi
tha
thing

WORD OF THE PAGE ▶ Notebook

'Just the people we were hoping to meet!' says the woman. 'I'm Wanda Write-a-lot, and this is Jimmy Snapshot. We're from *GO AWAY!* magazine and we've come to do a story on you!'

'Smile!' says Jimmy Snapshot, pointing his camera at us. CLICK!

CHAPTER 4

PENTS, PAXES AND PEPPER GRINDERS

'Are we there yet?' asks Terry for the fifty thousandth time, just as we arrive at the campsite.

'We sure are,' I say, getting out and taking a deep breath. 'Smell that fresh air!'

DEFINITION ▶ *The sound that Jimmy Snapshot's camera makes*

CLICK! Jimmy takes a photo of us breathing the fresh air.

'Do you like fresh air?' asks Wanda, her pen poised above her notebook.

'Of course!' I say. 'Doesn't everybody?'

WORD OF THE PAGE ▷ Photo

'I'm the one doing the interview, so I'll ask the questions if you don't mind,' she replies.

'Okay,' I say. Although I *do* mind. She's been asking questions and writing in her notebook the whole way here.

Edward and Mary climb out of their trailer.

'Oh, it's lovely,' says Mary, looking around. 'What's that big, shiny, watery thing?'

'That's a lake,' I say.

'Oh, it's lovely,' says Mary. 'Isn't it lovely, Edward?'

'Yes, it is,' he agrees, but he's not even looking at the lake—he's staring at Mary.

'What exactly happens on a camping holiday?' says Fancy Fish. 'I can't see a luxury hotel anywhere.'

WORD OF THE PAGE   Lake

'That's because there isn't one,' I explain.
'Camping holidays are all about putting up your
own shelter, doing your own cooking and making
your own fun.'

'But we didn't bring any of that stuff,' says Pinchy.
'You didn't tell us to.'

'Don't worry,' I say. 'You can share ours. Terry
has packed everything we need.'

'Yes,' says Terry. 'It's all right here.'

'Okay,' I say. 'First things first. Let's get the tent set up.'

'Tent?' says Terry.

'Yes, the tent. You did pack it, didn't you?'

'No,' says Terry.

'But I specifically asked if you'd packed the tent!' I say.

'Oh!' says Terry. 'I thought you said, "Have you *tacked the pent*?"'

'But that doesn't make any sense!' I say.

'I know,' says Terry. 'That's what I thought. So I packed one of these instead.'

He pulls a really big pepper grinder out of the back of the truck.

'Well?' says Terry proudly, giving the grinder a few turns. Pepper goes everywhere in a great black cloud. 'What do you think? I got it from the SUPER BIG STUFF storey.'

'Great!' I say. 'But it's not a tent, is it?'

'No, but it *rhymes* with tent.'

'It does not!' I say. 'It's a pepper grinder! Pepper grinder doesn't rhyme with tent!'

'It does if you use your imagination!' insists Terry.

'No it doesn't!' I say.

'Uh-oh!' says Edward. 'The pepper has gotten into The Trunkinator's trunk! I think he's going to sneeze!'

The Trunkinator unfolds the biggest handkerchief
I've ever seen and holds it up to his trunk.

We brace ourselves for the blast ...

A good friend of salt

but nothing happens.

'It's okay,' says Terry. 'False alarm!'

That's a relief!

'Hey, Trunky,' I say, 'if you're not going to use that handkerchief, can we borrow it?'

The Trunkinator shrugs and hands it over.

'Thanks,' I say. 'Everybody grab a corner, stretch it out and hold it up as high as you can. Terry, you put the giant pepper grinder in the middle—it will make a perfect centre pole!'

Mary pegs the corners and sides of the handkerchief into the ground with lollipop sticks and we soon have a tent that's big enough to hold everybody.

'Great work, team,' I say. 'Making do with what you have is what camping's all about! Okay, now all we need to do is chop some wood and make a fire. Can you give me the axe, Terry?'

'*Axe?*' says Terry.

'You did pack it, didn't you?'

'Um … no … you didn't tell me to.'

'Yes, I did,' I say. 'I specifically asked if you'd packed the axe.'

'Oh!' says Terry, striking his forehead. 'I thought you said, "Have you *acked the pax*?"'

'Of course you did,' I sigh.

'Did you really say that?' asks Wanda.

'No!' I shout. 'Because there's no such thing as a *pax*!'

'Yes there is,' says Terry, producing an axe. 'I have one right here.'

What Andy asked Terry to pack

'That's not a *pax*,' I say. 'It's an axe!'
'No,' says Terry. 'It's a *pax*.'

'Axe!'

'Pax!'

'Pax!'

'Axe!'

WORD OF THE PAGE ▶ Pax

'All right, all right,' I say. 'I give up. *Pax*, axe, whatever! Just hand it over—and stand clear.'

'How come you always get to chop the wood?' says Terry.

'Because I'm better at it than you,' I say.

'That's because you never let me have a go,' says Terry. 'How can I get better if you never let me practise?'

DEFINITION ▶ *Terry's word for 'axe'*

'That's a very good question,' says Wanda. 'I was just about to ask it myself. You're quite bossy, Andy, aren't you?'

CLICK!

'I'm not bossy,' I say. 'I just don't want any accidents. But fine, you can chop the wood, Terry. Just be careful!'

'Thanks, Andy,' says Terry. 'You can count on me. Can you hold the wood still for me?'

'Sure,' I say.

Terry swings, misses the wood, and the axe splits me right down the middle.

'OUCH!' says my right half. 'Now look what you've done—there's two of me!'

'You mean two of *us*!' says my left half.

'Smile, Andys!' says Jimmy. CLICK!

'How does it feel to be split in half with an axe?' says Wanda.

'How do you think?' we say.

CLICK!

'I'll ask the questions, remember?' says Wanda.

'Sorry,' we say. 'We forgot.'

'I'm sorry, too, Andy,' says Terry. 'I mean … Andys.'

'Never mind,' we say. 'Pass us the first-aid kit.'

'I didn't pack the first-aid kit,' says Terry. 'But I did pack this giant stapler from the SUPER BIG STUFF storey.'

CLICK!
CLICK!
CLICK!
CLICK!

'Well, we guess that will have to do,' we say.

'This won't hurt a bit,' says Terry as he staples me together again.

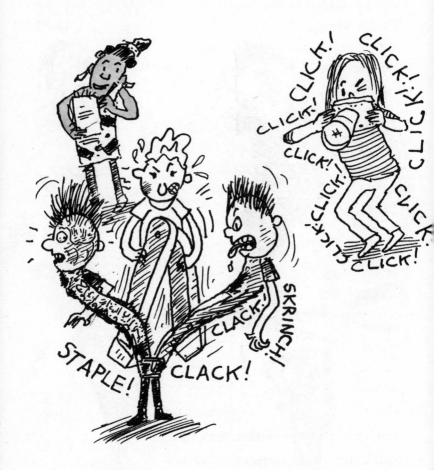

(I don't know if you've ever been chopped in half and stapled together again, but if you have, I'm sure you'd agree that it hurts ... A LOT!)

WORD OF THE PAGE ▷ Hurt

Finally my two halves are one again.

'There you go, Andy,' says Terry. 'As good as new!'

I am feeling surprisingly good, actually, apart from being quite hungry.

Turns out I'm not the only one.

'Excuse me, Andy,' says the kind scarecrow. 'I'm starving—is there anything to eat?'

'Of course there is,' I say. 'I asked Terry to pack lots of food.'

'Food?' says Terry.

'Yes, you did pack it, didn't you?' I say.

'Yes,' says Terry, looking uncertain.

'Really?' I say.

'No,' says Terry.

'Are you kidding me?' I say. 'I don't believe it! Thank goodness Edward and Mary brought their ice-cream and lollipop vendor trays.'

WORD OF THE PAGE ▶ Food

'I'm sorry, Andy,' says Edward. 'But there are no ice-creams or lollipops left. They were all eaten on the way here.'

'Well, that's great,' I say. 'Just great.'

'Relax, Andy,' says Terry.

'How can I relax if there's nothing to eat?' I shout.

'Don't worry,' says Terry. 'I packed fishing rods and a boat. We can go fishing and catch our dinner.'

'Actually, that's a pretty good idea,' I say. 'After all, fishing is a nice relaxing activity.'

'Unless you're a fish,' says Fancy Fish.

CHAPTER 5

ROW, ROW, ROW YOUR BOAT

Half an hour later, Terry and I are on a boat in the middle of the lake, fishing. Sure, it's relaxing, but it's not *quite* as relaxing as I'd hoped because ...

EVERYBODY ELSE IS ON THE BOAT TOO!!!

We are packed in like sardines, which is kind of funny, really, because sardines are what we're using for bait.

But there's nothing especially funny—or very relaxing—about fishing on a boat built for two with an inquisitive reporter, a snap-happy photographer, two enthusiastic robots, an enormous boxing elephant, a kind scarecrow, three talkative owls, a pinchy crab, a fancy fish and a bunch of overexcited penguins jumping around, playing badminton and trying to steal our bait.

We're all squashed together so tightly there's barely room to cast our lines in. To make matters worse, the boat is so low in the water that it feels like we could sink at any moment.

'BARAAAAAAAGH!' trumpets The Trunkinator, and he blasts a fountain of water into the air for the penguins to play in.

'Do that again!' says Jimmy, snapping away.

The Trunkinator doesn't need any encouragement.

'BARAAAAAAAAAAAGH!'

The penguins fly even higher this time.

WORD OF THE PAGE ▷ Baraaaaaagh

'I thought this was supposed to be a luxury cruise,' says Fancy Fish. 'Not a floating water park!'

'Oh, do cheer up, Fancy, you old stick-in-the-mud,' says Pinchy, clacking his pincers together in Fancy Fish's face. 'We're supposed to be having a holiday, and holidays are supposed to be fun!'

'Smile!' says Jimmy. CLICK!

Despite the crowded conditions, everybody (apart from Fancy Fish, that is) seems to be having a good time, especially Edward and Mary, who are so happy they start singing a song together.

'Row, row, row your boat,
Gently down the stream,
Merrily, merrily, merrily, merrily,
Life is but a dream!

Row, row, row your boat,
Gently down the stream.
If you see a crocodile,
Give it some ice-cream!

Row, row, row your boat,
Row and never stop.
If you're getting hungry,
Then suck a lollipop!'

'Row, row, row your boat,
Gently on the lake.
Don't forget to bring along
A really big—'

'CHEESECAKE!' shouts one of the three wise owls.

'Do you *like* cheesecake?' says Wanda.

'TRACTOR TYRE!' yells the second wise owl.

'I see,' says Wanda, noting it down. '*Tractor tyre cheesecake*—that's *very* interesting. Anything you'd like to add?'

'POOP POOP!' says the third wise owl.

With the noise of The Trunkinator's trumpeting, the excited chirps and squeals of the penguins, the clacking of Pinchy's pincers, the shouting of the wise owls, the clicking of Jimmy's camera, Edward and Mary's robotic singing, and Wanda's endless questions, I don't think there's much chance of us catching any fish.

But then I feel something on the end of my line. Something tugging. Something BIG!

'I think I've got something!' I shout.

'Hold it!' says Jimmy. CLICK!

'What do you think it is?' says Wanda, her pen at the ready.

'I don't know,' I say, 'but it sure is strong!'

'Do you like fishing? What's the biggest fish you ever caught? Has a fish ever caught *you*?'

I don't have time to answer Wanda's questions because whatever is on the end of the line is pulling really hard. In fact, it's pulling so hard it starts dragging the boat through the water.

'Hold on tight, everybody!' I say. 'Looks like we're going for a ride!'

'Yay!' says Terry as we zoom all over the lake. 'This is the best holiday ever!'

The boat gradually slows down. Whatever is pulling us must be getting tired. I start reeling it in.

There's a dark shape just below the surface of the water.

'It's a shark!' shouts Edward.

'It's not a shark,' says Mary. 'It's a bunyip.'

'It's not a shark *or* a bunyip,' says Terry. 'It's a bunyip-shark!'

I give one last big tug …

and it comes flying out of the water and lands on the deck of the boat with a big splash.

Everybody gasps.

And then un-gasps as we realise what it is.

It's not a shark …
or a bunyip …
or a bunyip-shark.

It's a boot.

A soggy old boot.

'Relax, everybody,' says Terry. 'It's just a soggy old boot.'

'Thank goodness!' says the kind scarecrow. 'Soggy old boots aren't dangerous.'

'Not normally,' I say, as I notice water pouring over the side of the boat and pooling around our legs. 'But this one might be. It's an extra bit of weight we definitely do not need.'

As I feared, the boat is sinking …

WORD OF THE PAGE   Sinking

lower …

and lower …

and lower …

and lower …

until it's completely sunk and we're all just floating in the water.

'Well, I guess that's the end of our fishing trip,' I say.

'Seems that way,' says Terry. 'But look on the bright side: swimming is very relaxing.'

'Especially if you're a fish,' says Fancy Fish.

'But not if you're a crab,' grumbles Pinchy.

WORD OF THE PAGE Swimming

CHAPTER 6

CAMPFIRE FUN

CLICK!

We all swim to the edge of the lake and make it back onto land—even the old boot.

'Lucky I packed my waterproof camera,' says Jimmy, pointing it at the boot. CLICK!

'And I'm glad I brought my waterproof notebook,' says Wanda.

She crouches beside the boot and starts asking it questions. 'How long have you been a boot? Who was your owner? Do you like being a boot? Do you like swimming? How long have you been in the lake?'

WORD OF THE PAGE Boot

'Hey, Andy,' says Terry. 'Look, Wanda is trying to interview the boot!'

'Wanda is such a great interviewer that she can get information out of anything,' says Jimmy. 'Animal, mineral, vegetable or, in this case, footwear!'

'Please be quiet,' says Wanda. 'I'm trying to conduct an interview.'

'Sorry,' I whisper. 'Come on, everybody, let's leave Wanda and the boot in peace and go make a fire to dry ourselves and warm up.'

DEFINITION ▶ *A boot-shaped shoe*

I use the pax to chop some wood and build a fire
(without splitting myself—or anybody else—
in half).

Soon we are all sitting around a blazing campfire.
We're warmer than we were, but still hungry.

WORD OF THE PAGE Hungry

'Can you eat soggy old boots?' says the kind scarecrow.

'Well, I guess you could,' I say. 'But I don't see why you'd want to.'

'Can you eat fire?' says Terry.

'Fire-eaters can,' I say. 'But it's dangerous. Remember the time we tried it?'

'Oh yeah,' says Terry. 'My tongue was on fire for weeks!'

HORSE-HEAD DUMPLINGS!

'The main thing campfires are good for,' I say, 'apart from warmth, is toasting marshmallows.'

'Did you bring the marshmallow machine?' says Pinchy.

'That's another thing Terry forgot to pack,' I say.

'You didn't ask me to pack it,' says Terry.

'Yes I did,' I say.

'No you didn't!'

'Yes—' I can't finish my sentence because a marshmallow has landed in my mouth. The marshmallow machine is hovering right in front of me!

'Looks like the marshmallow machine came anyway,' says Terry. 'Guess it needed a holiday, too.'

A stick dispenser pops out of the marshmallow machine, and soon we are all happily toasting marshmallows, even the old boot.

'This sure beats toasting marshmallows in our volcano,' says Terry.

'Totally!' I say. 'Remember that time it erupted all over us?'

'Yeah,' says Terry. 'That was funny.'

'No it wasn't,' I say. 'We got covered in super-hot lava!'

'Oh yeah,' says Terry. 'NOT funny.'

We toast marshmallows until everybody has had their fill and then we all settle back contentedly and look up at the stars.

This is turning out to be a pretty good holiday after all.

'The stars are so clear out here,' says Terry. 'I can see the Big Dipper.'

'I can see the big lollipop,' says Mary.

WORD OF THE PAGE ▶ Stars

'I can see the big ice-cream cone!' says Edward.

'I can see the big scarecrow!' says the kind scarecrow.

'QUAZJEX!' says the first wise owl.

'CORKSCREW!' says the second wise owl.

'BIG NOSE!' says the third.

'I can see the big dumdum!' I say, pointing at Terry.

'I can see an even bigger dumdum!' says Terry, pointing at me.

'Okay, that's enough stargazing for one night,' I say. 'Let's tell spooky campfire stories instead.'

'I love spooky campfire stories!' says Terry. 'Can I start? I've got a really spooky one.'

We all settle in.

Terry shines a torch up underneath his chin—
to give his face that spooky there's-a-torch-under-
my-chin look—and starts his story.

 'My spooky story is about a witch …

and a big, fat, hairy spider …

 and a full moon with a dark cloud passing across it.

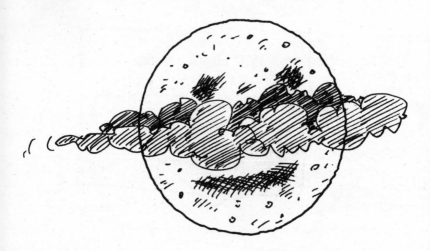

There's also a vampire puppy …

 a zombie kitten …

a haunted peanut-butter sandwich …

 a mysterious floating head …

a screaming caterpillar that just screams and
screams and when you ask it to stop it just keeps
screaming and screaming and screaming and

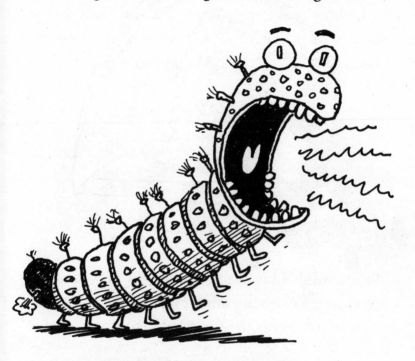

screaming and screaming and screaming and
screaming and screaming and screaming and
screaming and screaming and screaming and
screaming and screaming and screaming and
screaming and screaming and screaming and
screaming and screaming and screaming and
screaming and screaming and scream—'

'Terry!' I say. 'Is there any chance you could stop telling us *about* the story and start telling us the actual story?'

'I wish I could,' says Terry, 'but the scariest thing of all is that I can't remember it. All I know is that there's a witch. And a big, fat, hairy—'

'Never mind,' I say. 'I've got a scary story—and I'm pretty sure I can remember every word.'

Terry passes me the torch and I begin.

'In a dark, dark wood …

 there was a dark, dark house.

And in that dark, dark house, there was a dark, dark door.

 And behind that dark, dark door there was a dark, dark staircase.

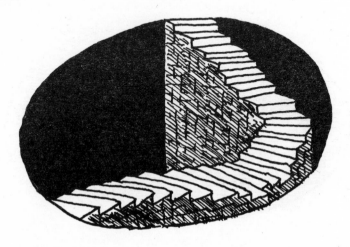

WORD OF THE PAGE ▶ Door

And at the top of that dark, dark staircase, there was a dark, dark room.

 And in that dark, dark room, there was a dark, dark box.

'And in that dark, dark box, there was a …'
(I pause for dramatic effect.)

'Tub of ice-cream?' says Edward.

'No,' I say. 'It wasn't a *refrigerated* box.'

'Melted ice-cream?' says Edward.

'No,' I say. 'There was no ice-cream, not frozen or melted … Besides, this is a spooky story and ice-cream isn't spooky!'

'A lollipop?' says Mary.

'No!' I say. 'Lollipops aren't spooky either!'

'A dot?' says Terry.

'NO!' I say. 'Stop trying to wreck my story. Dots are the least spooky thing in the whole world!'

'Well, what *was* in the box, then?' says Wanda.

I take a deep breath. 'It was a …

CHAPTER 7

FRED THE GHOSTLY GHOST

'Why are you shouting, Andy?' says Terry.

'Because I'm trying to scare you,' I say. 'Pretty scary, huh?'

'Not really,' says Terry. 'Ghosts aren't real. And even if they were, they wouldn't scare *me*.'

'Actually, ghosts *are* real,' says the kind scarecrow, 'and they can be *quite* scary. Did I ever tell you the story of Fred the ghostly ghost?'

'I don't think so,' says Terry. 'But a story about a ghost called *Fred* doesn't *sound* very scary.'

'I can assure you it is,' says the scarecrow. 'In fact, it's probably far too frightening to tell now when we're all alone out here in the woods in the dark.'

WORD OF THE PAGE ▶ Frightening

'I've never heard a ghost story,' says Mary Lollipoppins. 'But I'm sure I'd like it. I won't be scared.'

'Me neither,' says Edward. 'Robots don't get scared.'

'Please tell us about Fred,' I say.

'I'm not sure if I can,' says the scarecrow. 'I'm a kind scarecrow and it wouldn't be kind to scare people with a spooky ghost story.'

'But it would be kind to tell people a spooky ghost story if they really wanted you to,' I say.

'Especially if they said please,' says Terry. 'Pleeeeeeeeeeeeeeeeeeeeeeeeeeeeeeeeeeeeeeeeeeeeeeeeeeeeeeeeeeeeeeease?'

'Pretty please?' says Fancy Fish.

'Pretty please with lollipops on top?' says Mary.

'And ice-cream?' says Edward.

The scarecrow shrugs. 'All right,' it says. 'I'll tell you, but I'll try to make it a bit less scary.'

We all lean forward. I pass the torch and the scarecrow begins speaking in a low voice.

'It was a dark and stormy night.'

Terry gasps, his eyes wide.

'Well,' says the kind scarecrow, noticing Terry's fright, 'when I say "dark", I don't mean *dark* dark. It was quite light actually. In fact, to tell you the truth, it wasn't even night-time. It was the middle of the day. And there was no storm—just a light and pleasant summery breeze.'

'Oh, thank goodness,' says Terry. 'That was getting kind of scary. But where's Fred? When does he come into the story?'

'Right now,' says the scarecrow. 'One pleasant summer's day, Fred went to bed—'

'He went to bed in the middle of the day?' says Pinchy. 'That's weird.'

'Yes,' says the scarecrow. 'Fred was weird, but he was also quite tired. He only intended to have a short nap but when he got into bed he bumped his head—'

'Did he bump it hard?' says Wanda, taking notes. She looks concerned.

'No,' says the scarecrow quickly, 'not too hard. Just a little bump.'

'I see,' says Wanda. 'And what happened next?'

'Well,' says the scarecrow, 'Fred slept all day and he slept all night and then he couldn't get up in the morning.'

Lets eat that man.

'Because he was still tired?' says Edward.

'No,' says the scarecrow. 'Because he was dead.'

Terry gasps. 'Dead?!' he says. 'But … why?'

'The doctors were uncertain,' says the scarecrow, 'but they concluded that the most likely cause of death was the bump to the head.'

'But you said it was just a little bump,' says Mary.

'It was,' says the scarecrow, 'but Fred had a very soft head.'

'How soft?' says Wanda.

'*Quite* soft,' says the scarecrow.

'So he died?' says Terry.

'I'm afraid so,' says the scarecrow. 'He became a ghost. "Whooo, whooo," said Fred, as he floated up into the air, out the window, over the hills and far away.'

'How far away?' says Wanda.

'Far *far* away,' says the scarecrow.

'That's quite a nice story,' says Terry, 'and not too scary at all. I love stories with happy endings.'

'So do I,' says the scarecrow, 'but unfortunately, that isn't the end.'

'What happened after he became a ghost?' says Terry.

'Well,' says the scarecrow, 'then Fred was blown into the blades of a wind turbine.'

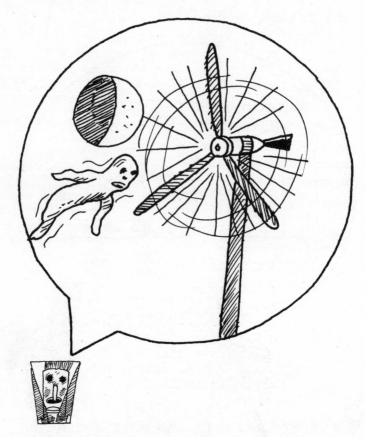

'Oh dear,' says Fancy Fish. 'Was he all right?'

'Not really,' says the scarecrow. 'He was chopped into lots of tiny pieces.'

'Blimey!' says Pinchy. 'Don't tell me he died again!'

'He did indeed,' says the scarecrow. 'He *double-died*.'

'But that would make him the ghost of a ghost!' I say. 'Is that even possible?'

'Not only possible,' says the scarecrow, 'but that's exactly what happened. And then it got even worse.'

'Worse?' says Terry. 'How?'

'Because,' says the scarecrow, 'then the ghost of Fred's ghost was blown into a river—a big wet one—and drowned ... *drowned to death*!'

'The ghost *drowned*?' says Wanda.

'I'm afraid so,' says the scarecrow. 'Ghosts can do a lot of things, but they can't swim. Fred the ghost of a ghost became the ghost of a ghost ... of a *ghost*! And then—'

'Okay, thanks, Scarecrow,' I say, stepping in before the ghost of a ghost of a ghost story can become any scarier, or any more confusing. 'I think that's enough spooky stories for one evening. It's probably time we all went to bed.'

'Wait,' says Terry. 'What's that noise?'

'What noise?' I say.

'That rustling noise,' says Terry. 'In the woods. Listen!'

WORD OF THE PAGE ▶ Listen

CHAPTER 8

WE'RE NOT SCARED!

CLICK!

We all freeze.

There's someone—or some*thing*—in the woods!

DEFINITION ▶ *Something you can do with your ears*

'I hope it's not Fred the ghostly ghost,' says Mary.

'I hope it *is*,' says Jimmy. 'I'd love to get a shot of a ghost of a ghost of a ghost!'

'It's getting louder!' says Pinchy.

WORD OF THE PAGE Ghostly

RUSTLE!

'It's getting closer!' says Fancy Fish.

RUSTLE!

'Somebody needs to go and investigate,' I say.
'I nominate Terry.'

'And I nominate *you*,' says Terry.

'Too late,' I say. 'I nominated you first.'

'I know,' says Terry. 'But I think you should go. You're a narrator. You'll be able to describe whatever it is much better than I could.'

'True, but you're an illustrator. You'll be able to draw a picture of whatever it is, and you know what they say—a picture is worth a thousand words.'

'You're just saying that because you're scared,' says Terry.

'And you're just saying that because *you're* scared,' I say.

'It sounds to me like you're *both* scared,' says Wanda.

'I'm not scared,' I say. 'Not a bit.'

'Me neither,' says Terry. 'I'm not scared of *anything*!'

'I find that hard to believe,' says Wanda. 'For instance, what if a really hungry lion was running towards you? Surely you'd be scared then.'

'Not me,' I say. 'I'd just yawn.'

'I wouldn't even bother yawning,' says Terry. 'That's how *un*-scared I would be.'

WORD OF THE PAGE ▶ Un-scared

'But wouldn't you be scared of being eaten?' says Wanda.

'No,' says Terry. 'I might end up being eaten, sure, but I wouldn't be scared.'

'Me neither,' I say. 'Being eaten is nothing to be scared of.'

'What about looking up and seeing a huge meteor coming towards you and realising you're about to get smashed to smithereens?' says Wanda. 'I bet you'd be scared then.'

'No,' I say.

'Not at all,' says Terry. 'Meteors just make me laugh.'

WORD OF THE PAGE ▶ Smithereens

'All right,' says Wanda. 'How about this: what if you were about to be eaten by a lion that was riding a meteor that was about to smash into you? Would you be scared *then*?'

'Nope,' I say.

'Nope,' says Terry.

'Nope?' says Wanda.

'Nope,' I say. 'Because we're not scared of *anything*, are we, Terry?'

'Nope,' he says. 'Nothing at all!'

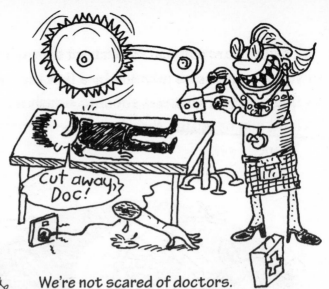

 We're not scared of doctors.

We're not scared of dentists.

We're not scared of pharmacists—

or nurses or hygienists.

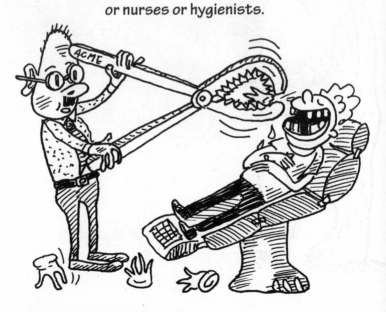

We're not scared of having fights
with bears with buns and fridges.
We're not scared of crossing over
flimsy, narrow bridges.

We're not scared of zombies,
or dinosaurs that roar,

or of spooky, severed arms
that creep across the floor.

We're not scared of haunted houses
full of ghouls and ghosts.
We really are not scared at all—
these aren't just empty boasts.

We're not scared
of taking a test
or of being trapped
in a giant bird's nest.

I haven't a clue!

YUM!

We're not scared
of witches and wizards,
or gizzards
or blizzards
or scissors
or lizards!

Z

Andy

Crocodile

We're not scared
of mud and dirt,
of cuts and bruises
or getting hurt.

We're not scared
of deadly snakes
that slither, slide
and wriggle!

The thought of pain
just makes us grin
and smile and laugh
and giggle.

KLUNK!

Hey, that's a BEAR TRAP,
not an IDIOT TRAP!

SNAP!

We have no fear
of dangling spiders,
reckless drivers,
elephant bikers,
hungry tigers,
smelly diapers
or being chased
by ghostly riders.

SPLAT!

It doesn't matter what it is,
if it is big or small,
We're not scared—
Oh no, we're not.
Nope! We're not scared at all!

DEFINITION ▶ *People (or elephants) who ride bikes*

'That's great!' says Jimmy. 'Since neither of you are scared of anything, then why don't you go and investigate what the noise is?'

'What noise?' I say. 'I can't hear any noise. Can you, Terry?'

'No,' says Terry. 'Whatever it was, I think it's gone.'

'THAT noise!' says Wanda.

WORD OF THE PAGE ▶ Noise

'Oh, you mean that n-n-noise,' I say. 'I g-guess we should g-go and investigate.'

'Y-y-yeah,' says Terry.

'All right then,' I say. 'L-l-let's!'

Terry and I slowly walk towards the woods.

As we enter the woods the rustling gets louder …

WORD OF THE PAGE ▶ RUSTLE!!!

Suddenly there's a flash of light.

'I think I can see it!' says Terry. 'It's got one eye! One bright shiny eye!'

'It's a Cyclops!' I shout. 'Run!'

But before I can move, I feel a hand—or is it a claw?—on my shoulder.

'Wait!' says a voice. 'It's me!'

'Wh-wh-who's m-m-me?' I say.

'Jill!' says the voice.

WORD OF THE PAGE Claw

CHAPTER 9

WE'RE GOING ON A HOBYAH HUNT!

'Jill?' I say. 'What are you doing here? And why are you dressed like that?'

'I'm on a hobyah hunt,' says Jill. 'What are you doing here?'

'We're on a camping holiday,' says Terry. 'This is our new camping ground level.'

'Oh, I didn't realise I'd climbed *your* tree,' says Jill. 'I was following some hobyah tracks through the forest and they led me here.'

'Come and see our campsite,' says Terry. 'We've got a tent and everything!'

'And *everyone*,' I say.

I introduce Jill to Jimmy and Wanda and explain to everyone that there was no need for them to be scared—the rustling in the bushes was just her.

'Yeah,' says Terry. 'She's hunting hobyahs … whatever *they* are.'

'You don't know what a hobyah is?' says Jill.
'Never heard of them,' says Terry.
'Me neither,' I say.

'Tell us more about these hobyahs,' says Wanda.
'I think our readers at *GO AWAY!* magazine will
be very interested in them.'

CLICK!

'Well,' says Jill, 'they're mysterious little creatures
that live in the woods. There have been many
sightings, but nobody can quite agree on what
they look like.'

Some say they look like lizards.
Some say they're more like cats.
Some say they're cute like rabbits.
Some say they're more like rats.

Some say they're like a possum ...
or a long-nosed potoroo.
The only thing we know for sure
is what they like to do:
they skip, skip, skip
on the tips of their toes
and sneak up on
you at night ...

← Toes →

skip   skip   skip   skip

They put you in a bag
and tie the bag up tight—
Then they hang it up on something,
high up off the ground,
and poke the bag with sticks
as they dance and jump around.

They shout, 'Hobyah! Hobyah! Hobyah!'
as they laugh and poke at you.
'Hobyah! Hobyah! Hobyah!'
they chant the whole night through.

But then, when the sun rises
they fall down
upon the ground.
And sleep soundly
through the daytime,
until the sun goes down.

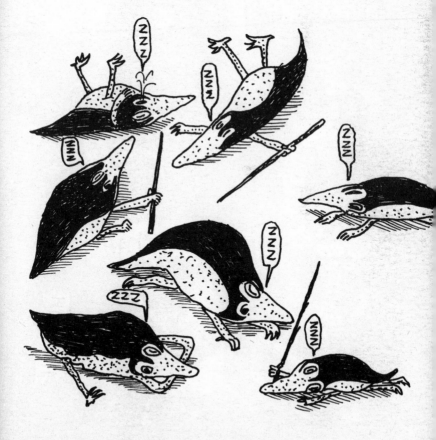

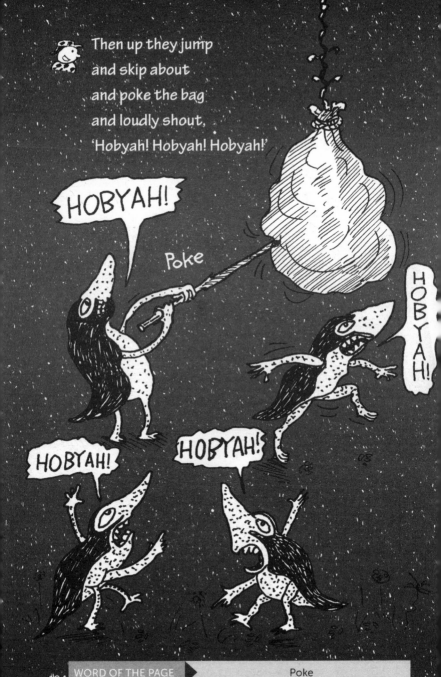

Then up they jump
and skip about
and poke the bag
and loudly shout,
'Hobyah! Hobyah! Hobyah!'

'They sound creepy,' I say. 'I'm glad there's none around here.'

'But I think there are,' says Jill. 'There are hobyah tracks all over these woods.'

'Have you ever seen a hobyah, Jill?' says Terry.

'No, but I'd sure like to. That's why I'm on a hobyah hunt.'

'I'd do *anything* to get a photo of one!' says Jimmy. 'It would be a world first!'

WORD OF THE PAGE ▶ Hunt

'And I'd really like to interview one,' says Wanda. 'What an amazing scoop that would be!'

'You should all join me on my hunt,' says Jill. 'I'm pretty sure there are some hobyahs around here, and close! I can practically smell them!'

'Hang on a minute,' I say. 'Hobyahs are kind of nasty, right?'

'Right,' says Jill. '*Really* nasty.'

'And horrible?' says Terry.

'Yep,' says Jill. '*Really* horrible.'

WORD OF THE PAGE ▶ Horrible

'And there's a strong chance they could catch us, put us in a bag, hang it up and poke us with sticks and yell "Hobyah! Hobyah! Hobyah!" and we'd be absolutely powerless to do anything about it?'

'Yes,' says Jill. 'A really, really, *really* strong chance. So, what do you think?'

'Hmmm,' I say.

'Hmmmmm,' says Terry.

'Well?' says Jill.

'Well …' I say. 'What are we waiting for? LET'S GO ON A HOBYAH HUNT!'

CHAPTER 10

A DARK, DARK HOUSE

'Wait!' says Jill. 'Not so fast. We need to stick together ... hobyahs can be dangerous.'

'So can I!' says Terry. 'If those hobyahs try to put me into a bag, they're going to regret it!'

'That's for sure,' I say. 'Come on, everybody, let's go!'

There's no response.
    'Everybody?'
    I look around.
    There's no one there.

'Have they all gone to bed?' says Terry.

'No,' I say. 'The tent's empty.'

'But if they're not here,' says Terry, 'then where are they?'

We look at each other and gasp.

'I think the hobyahs have got them,' says Jill.

'They've put them in bags!' I say.

'They'll poke them with sticks!' says Terry.

'And chant "Hobyah! Hobyah! Hobyah!",' says Jill. 'We've got to find them. I think I can see some fresh tracks ... follow me!'

I follow Jill.

I turn around to make sure Terry is following me, but I can't see him.

'Terry!' I call. 'This way!'

There's no response.

I call him again.

And again.

But he's gone.

WORD OF THE PAGE ▶ Gone

'Jill!' I shout. 'They've got Terry!'
  Silence.
  'Jill?' I say. 'Jill?'

'Jill?'
  Nothing.
  Oh no—they've got her too!
  Now I'm all alone.
  All alone in the woods without my friends and surrounded by hostile hobyahs!

But, hey, I'm fine.
 I'm not scared.
 I'm not scared a bit.
 Not one little teeny-tiny, itty-bitty …

All right, I admit it … I *am* scared!

REALLY

SCARED!!

SUPER

SCARED!!!

That's when I hear a noise.

Uh-oh. They're coming for me now!

I shut my eyes tight.

I can hear them getting closer … and closer … and closer.

They're right beside me. But they haven't grabbed me. They haven't put me in a bag. Why not? I open my eyes.

Because it's not the hobyahs. That's why not.

It's just the old boot.

Never in my life have I been so happy to see a soggy old boot.

'Old boot!' I say. 'I'm so happy to see you!'

The old boot doesn't reply, but I'm pretty sure it's happy to see me too.

The old boot hops ahead of me. Then it stops, as if it's waiting for me to catch up.

I shrug and follow it. I mean, it's not as if I have a whole lot of other options at this point.

WORD OF THE PAGE ▶ Shrug

I follow the old boot into the dark woods.
Or perhaps I should say the *dark, dark* woods.
And the deeper we go into the dark, dark woods,
the darker and darker they get!

Hop Hop Hop

We walk (well, I walk and the boot hops) for what
seems like a long time. Then I see a shadowy
outline.

It's a house.

A dark house.

A dark, dark house—just like the one in my story!

Actually, I know that house.

It's the haunted house on our haunted house level (the one we added when we built our 52-storey treehouse).

I follow the boot up the dark, dark steps to the dark, dark door.

As I stand there in front of the door, wondering whether to knock, the door slowly creaks open … all by itself!

I see a dark, dark staircase.

WORD OF THE PAGE ▶ Staircase

I can hear the chanting of hobyahs coming from upstairs. I don't want to go up there, but I have to save Terry and Jill and all our friends. Besides, the boot is already halfway up. I follow it.

I put my foot on the first stair—the first dark, dark stair ...

and then the stair after that ...

and the stair after that ...

until the boot and I are at the top of the dark, dark staircase, just outside a dark, dark room.

The chanting is loud now.

WORD OF THE PAGE HOBYAH!

CHAPTER 11

HOBYAH! HOBYAH! HOBYAH!

I peer into the room. It's big and dark, but I can see a huge chandelier hanging from the ceiling, and hanging from the chandelier are a bunch of bags.

A group of hobyahs are dancing around the bags, poking them with sticks and shouting, 'Hobyah! Hobyah! Hobyah!'

'Hey, quit it!' shouts Terry from inside one of the bags. 'You're going to be really sorry when my friend Andy finds out what you've done to us!'

'HOBYAH! HOBYAH! HOBYAH!' shout the hobyahs.

'We don't mean you any harm,' calls Jill. 'Can't you just let us out and we'll leave you in peace?'

'HOBYAH! HOBYAH! HOBYAH!' shout the hobyahs.

'Would it be possible for you to stop shouting "Hobyah! Hobyah! Hobyah!" so I can interview you?' calls Wanda. 'I think our readers would love to hear your story!'

'And if you give me back my camera, I'll take some photos of you!' yells Jimmy.

'HOBYAH! HOBYAH! HOBYAH!' chant the hobyahs in reply.

'Everyone's here and they're okay!'* I whisper to the boot. 'But how are we going to rescue them? We're completely outnumbered!'

*If your definition of 'okay' includes being strung up in a bag and poked with sticks.

I don't know if the boot can understand me or not. It's kind of hard to tell. But it must have understood something, because it rises up on its toe, hops rapidly into the room …

and starts kicking the hobyahs!

223

Hobyahs are flying everywhere, but as soon as they land, they pick themselves up, run back and attack the boot.

They all pile on top of it and hold it down. If I don't do something, the old boot will end up in a bag, just like the others.

As scared as I am, I can't let that happen.

I have to save it! I step through the doorway.

'Hold it right there,' I say.

WORD OF THE PAGE Something

The hobyahs stare at me.

I stare at the hobyahs.

'Put the boot down and step away from the bag,' I say.

But the hobyahs do not put the boot down, and they don't step away from the bag. They shove the boot into it and start moving towards me.

Uh-oh. Bad ... bad ... not good ... bad!

As the hobyahs come closer, I notice that it's getting easier to see them. There's more light in the room. That's because it's almost dawn. The sun is about to rise.

As it gets lighter, the hobyahs get slower ...

and slower ...

and sleepier ...

and sleepier ...

WORD OF THE PAGE ▶ Bad

until they all slump to the floor in a big heap, and start snoring loudly.

It's just like Jill said—they dance all night and sleep all day.

I tiptoe around the snoring hobyahs and untie
one of the bags.

Terry falls out and hits the ground with a
loud thud.

He lies there blinking for a moment, blinded by
the light. Then he jumps up and puts me in a
headlock.

'You hobyahs are going to be sorry for what
you did!' he says.

WORD OF THE PAGE   Thud

'Terry!' I say as loudly as I dare. 'I'm not a hobyah! It's me, Andy!'

'Andy?' says Terry, releasing me from the headlock. 'Why did you put me in a bag and poke me with a stick?'

'I didn't,' I say. 'The hobyahs did! They caught you back at the campfire and brought you to the haunted house level. I was lost in the woods for a while, but the old boot found me and led me here.'

'Where are the hobyahs now?' says Terry.

'All around us,' I say, pointing. 'They fell asleep as soon as the sun came up. Let's free the others and get out of here.'

WORD OF THE PAGE ▶ Sun

We move around as quietly as we can and let everyone out of the bags.

'Okay,' I whisper. 'Everybody follow the old boot. And be careful not to wake the hobyahs.'

We are tiptoeing towards the door when I hear a shout.

I turn and see Jimmy Snapshot having a tug of war with a hobyah that has hold of his camera.

'It's *my* camera!' shouts Jimmy. 'Let go!'

'HOBYAH!' shouts the hobyah, which I'm fairly sure in this case means 'NO!'

All the shouting is disturbing the other hobyahs. They're waking up, and—even worse—getting up, and creep-creep-creeping towards us on the tips of their creepy little toes. They surround us in a menacing ring.

'HOBYAH! HOBYAH! HOBYAH!' chant the hobyahs as they close in on us.

'What do we do now, Jill?' I say. 'Can you talk to them?'

'Unfortunately not,' says Jill. 'I can talk to almost every animal there is, but I can't talk to hobyahs. All they seem to want to do is shout "Hobyah!" I don't think I've ever encountered such unintelligent and unpleasant creatures— and I've met quite a few.'

WORD OF THE PAGE　　　Unpleasant

The hobyahs come closer …

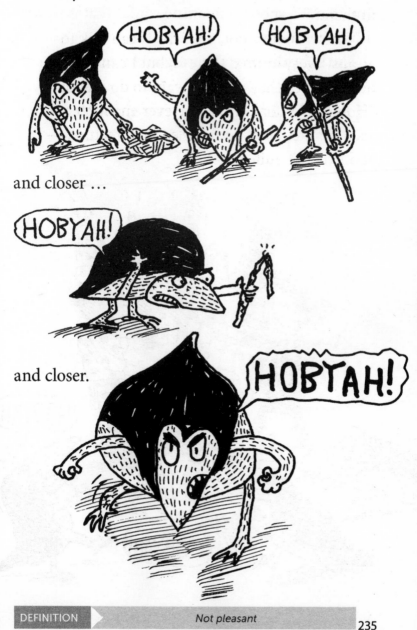

and closer …

and closer.

They are chanting loudly, but not loudly enough to drown out a spooky moaning sound that is slowly filling the room.

The hobyahs stop shouting and freeze.

Something that looks like a cloud of smoke—or a mist—appears in front of us. It slowly assumes the shape of a—

'Look!' says Terry. 'It's Fred! Fred the ghostly ghost!'

WORD OF THE PAGE ▸ Freeze

'Whoooo,' says Fred the ghostly ghost.

The hobyahs start backing away from us—and Fred—very slowly. They are obviously scared of ghosts.

'Are these hobyahs giving you any trouble?' says Fred.

'As a matter of fact they are,' I say. 'We're trying to get out of here, but they won't let us go.'

'Leave them to me,' says Fred. 'Ghosts and hobyahs are natural enemies. If there's one thing I like doing, it's going on a good old-fashioned hobyah *haunt*!'

Fred moans again very loudly …

WORD OF THE PAGE ▶ Haunt

and the hobyahs run for the door as fast as their creepy little toes can carry them!

Fred chases the hobyahs out of the dark, dark room …

down the dark, dark stairs …

out the dark, dark door …

down the dark, dark steps …

into the dark, dark woods …

and out the other side!

'Oh no!' says Terry. 'Now the treehouse will be full of hobyahs!'

'Maybe not,' says Jill. 'Look! They're heading straight towards the deep, dark cave—the one with the dragon in it!'

The hobyahs all run into the cave with Fred hot on their trail.

WHoooo!

We hear a loud roar, see a burst of flames, and then a cloud of foul-smelling smoke comes pouring out of the mouth of the cave.

'I guess that's the end of the hobyahs,' says Terry.

THIS IS A
CAVE
WARNING
SIGN

DANGER

M...GER
BAD
THINGS

An opening in a cave, or a face

'I guess it's the end of Fred, too,' I say.

'No it's not,' says Terry. 'Look! There he goes! He's the ghost of a ghost of a ghost of a ghost now!'

CHAPTER 12

WEDDING BEEPS

'I feel sorry for Fred,' says Jill, 'but I feel even sorrier for the hobyahs.'

'Are you kidding me?' I say. 'They tied you up in a bag, poked you with a stick and yelled "Hobyah!" at you over and over!'

'And not only that, but they stole my camera!' says
Jimmy. 'I've lost all of my what-were-sure-to-be-
award-winning photos!'

'And they stole my notebook and pen,' says
Wanda. 'All my notes. All my interviews. All
burned up by a dragon. Now we have no story!'

I hear a clanking sound and look around.

Mary and Edward have put their heads together and are whispering excitedly.

Edward looks up. 'Maybe Mary and I can help,' he says to Wanda. 'I think we might have a scoop for you!'

'Thanks, Edward,' says Wanda, 'but I don't feel like ice-cream at the moment. What I need is a story.'

'That's exactly what we're offering you,' says Mary.
'We're not talking about a scoop of ice-cream—
we're talking about *news*.'

Weddings make him cry.

'News?' says Wanda. 'What sort of news?'

'Edward and I have decided to get married,'
says Mary.

'That's wonderful!' I say. 'We've never had a wedding in the treehouse before.'

We all crowd around Edward and Mary and congratulate them.

'Can we throw nuts and bolts, instead of confetti?' says Terry.

'Of course,' says Edward. 'That's what happens at robot weddings.'

'That is definitely great news,' says Wanda. 'I'm very happy for you both. But, unfortunately, *GO AWAY!* magazine doesn't cover weddings—it's only about holidays.'

'We know!' says Mary. 'And that's what we're talking about—we would like to offer *GO AWAY!* magazine exclusive rights to our wedding *and* our honeymoon holiday!'

'Yes,' says Edward. 'We are going to Ye Olde Worlde Historical Village where we will feast on olde-fashioned ice-cream and lollipops, have

WORD OF THE PAGE ▶ Honeymoon

a carriage ride down the olde-fashioned main street, get our circuits tuned by an olde-fashioned technician and take part in an olde-fashioned bar room brawl in Ye Olde Historical Saloon!'

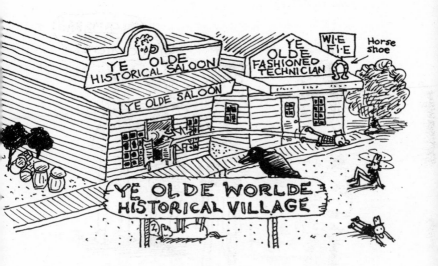

'I'm not sure about the olde-fashioned bar room brawl,' says Mary. 'I don't want anybody to get hurt.'

'Don't worry,' says Edward. 'We can't get hurt because we're robots, remember? And nobody else will get hurt because all the customers and staff are robots, too!'

'Well, in that case, let the olde-fashioned bar room brawling begin!' says Mary. 'So, what do you think, Wanda and Jimmy—are you in?'

'That would make a fantastic story,' says Wanda.
'And I'm sure our readers would love it. There's
just one problem—we don't have anything to
record it with. As you know, the hobyahs stole my
pen and notebook.'

'And my camera!' says Jimmy, looking like he's
about to cry. 'My beautiful, *award-winning*
camera!'

'Never fear!' says Fancy Fish, stepping forward.
'I have the finest selection of pens, pencils,
notebooks and award-winning cameras right here!'

Fancy Fish opens his coat to reveal cameras of all
shapes and sizes on one side and a vast selection of
notebooks and pens on the other.

If it's notebooks or pens
That you're looking for,
I have them right here
In my new pop-up store.

I have cameras a-plenty—
Every shape, every size—
In my two-million-dollar
Temporary enterprise.

If it's high prices you want,
And high prices you desire,
I can personally guarantee
You won't find any higher!

'That's amazing!' says Jimmy, looking at the cameras. 'I'd like this one, please.'

'And this pen and notebook set will suit me just fine,' says Wanda.

'Excellent,' says Fancy Fish. 'I admire your taste. That will be two million dollars each.'

DIGITAL CAMERA

Super pen

NOTE BOOK

2M...

2,000,000 price tag

$2M

'Darn,' says Jimmy. 'I only have two dollars.'

'Me too,' says Wanda sadly.

'Never fear,' says Pinchy. 'I have my own pop-up Two-Dollar Shop right here—nothing over two dollars. I can sell you each two million dollars for just *two* dollars each.'

'Thanks, Pinchy,' says Wanda.

'Yeah, thanks, Pinchy,' says Jimmy. 'You're a lifesaver!'

'I'm a crab, actually,' says Pinchy. 'But always happy to help.'

WORD OF THE PAGE   Lifesaver

'Okay, we're ready!' says Wanda. 'When is the wedding?'

'Right now!' says Mary.

At that moment, the wedding march starts to play and a robot wedding celebrant rolls in.

The robot celebrant says, 'We are gathered here today for the wedding of two of the sweetest robots in the treehouse. Do you, Mary and Edward, take each other to have and to hold, to oil and maintain with regular updates for as long as you both shall function?'

WORD OF THE PAGE   Celebrant

'We do,' say Edward and Mary.

'I now pronounce you Robot and Robot!'

We all throw handfuls of nuts and bolts at Edward and Mary as they leave in Edward's ice-cream van, which the penguins have decorated.

WORD OF THE PAGE ▶ Throw

GULP!

A fun thing to do with your hands

265

Trailing behind are Wanda, asking questions and jotting down the answers with her two-million-dollar pen and notebook set, and Jimmy, snapping away happily with his new two-million-dollar camera.

CHAPTER 13

THE LAST CHAPTER

'Well that was a nice holiday!' says Terry.

'Yes,' I say. 'It wasn't quite as relaxing as I'd hoped, but it was exciting and it *has* given us plenty to write about for the next book.'

'*And* we got to see some hobyahs,' says Jill.

'*And* the ghost of a ghost of a ghost of a ghost!' says Terry. 'Let's write it all down and draw the pictures before we forget a single thing!'

We write …

and draw …

and draw …

and write …

and draw …

'Yay!' says Terry as we zoom all over the lake. 'This is the best holiday ever!'

108   109

and draw …

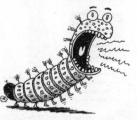

PEn
guiN

a haunted peanut-butter sandwich …

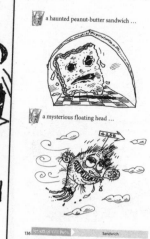

a mysterious floating head …

a screaming caterpillar that just screams and screams and when you ask it to stop it just keeps screaming and screaming and screaming and

screaming and screaming and screaming and
screaming and screaming and screaming and
screaming and screaming and screaming and
screaming and screaming and screaming and
screaming and screaming and screaming and
screaming and screaming and screaming and
screaming and screaming and screaming and
screaming and screaming and scream—'

136   Sandwich

What a sandwich-making machine makes   137

and write …

ABcdEfgH

and write …

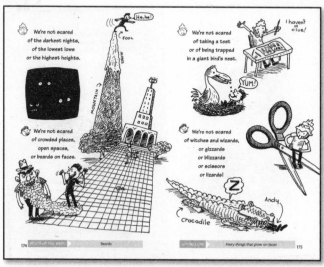

hesaid
She
said
they
said
we
said
it
said
that
I said
we
all
said

and draw …

and write …

and write …

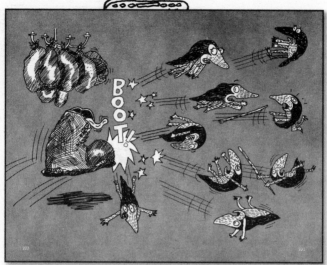

and draw …

until it's all finished!

'Perfect!' I say. 'The best one yet! But it's taken longer than I thought. The book is due at Mr Big Nose's office in 45 seconds! How on Earth are we going to get it there on time?'

The old boot starts clomping around noisily.

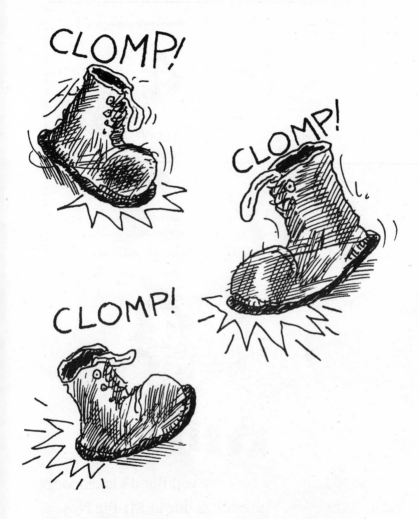

'I think it's trying to tell us something,' says Jill.
'And I think I know exactly what it is,' I say.

I put the book on the edge of the deck and the boot hops up behind it and gives it a really hard kick … and when I say 'a really hard kick', I mean a really, REALLY hard kick!

WORD OF THE PAGE ▶ Kick

The book flies up, up and away ...

across the forest …

WORD OF THE PAGE Forest

over the city …

WORD OF THE PAGE ▶ City

and down into Mr Big Nose's office.

WORD OF THE PAGE ▸ Office

'Great kick!' I say to the old boot.

'That's some boot,' says Terry. 'Can it stay with us here in the treehouse?'

'Sure,' I say. 'I've grown quite fond of it!'

'Yay!' says Terry. 'I've always wanted an old boot level, and if we find any other old boots, they can live there, too!'

A lot of leaves →

'Knock, knock!' calls a voice from below.

'Who's there?' says Terry.

'Bill!'

'Bill who?' says Terry.

'Bill the postman!'

'Bill the postman who?' says Terry.

'It's not a knock-knock joke, Terry,' calls Bill. 'It's *me*—Bill the postman! I've got a delivery for you.'

'Oh! Sorry, Bill,' says Terry, and we all go down to open the door.

'Special delivery,' says Bill, handing us a magazine. 'If I'm not mistaken, it's the latest issue of *GO AWAY!* with Edward and Mary on the cover!'

GO AWAY!
MAGAZINE

MECHANICAL SWEETHEARTS TIE THE NUT!

EXCLUSIVE

ye-olde worlde
historical
village
honeymoon
holiday

PICS INSIDE

WORDS BY WANDA WRITE-A-LOT • PHOTOS BY JIMMY SNAPSHOT

'Well, that all worked out really well,' says Terry. 'What should we do now?'

'I think we should add another 13 storeys to the treehouse,' I say.

'And make it 156-storeys?' says Terry. 'Cool! I've always *wanted* a 156-storey treehouse.'

'We'll be needing an old boot level for the old boot to live on, for a start,' I say.

'And an aquarium wonderland for Quazjex,' says Terry. 'In fact, I've made a little plan here.'

WORD OF THE PAGE   Aquarium

'Quazjex?' says Jill. 'What's that?'

'It's my new pet axolotl,' says Terry.

'It's okay, Terry,' I say. 'You don't have to keep pretending that you have a pet axolotl called Quazjex. I don't care that you made it up. I'm not angry anymore. Despite our completely non-relaxing holiday, I feel quite relaxed.'

'I didn't make it up,' says Terry, pointing at the sky. 'Look! Here's Quazjex now.'

I look up and, sure enough, an axolotl wearing a little cape is flying towards us.

'Why is it wearing a cape?' says Jill.

'Because Quazjex is no *ordinary* axolotl,' says Terry. It's a *stunt* axolotl!'

It lands on the deck and says, '*Hola, mi nombre es Quazjex.*'

Oh no—I don't believe it!

Quazjex is real?!

I think I need another holiday!

Lots of laughs

at every level!

Lots of laughs

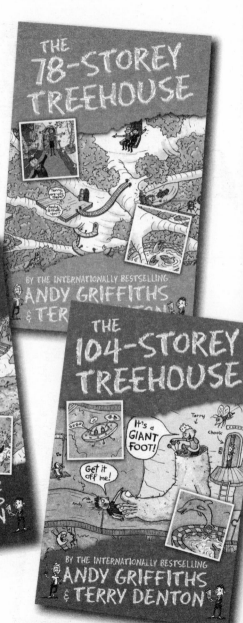

at every level!

Lots of laughs at every level!